2
1
26
17

For Mum

First published 2009 by Walker Books Ltd
87 Vauxhall Walk, London SE11 5HJ

2 4 6 8 10 9 7 5 3 1

© 2009 Polly Dunbar

The right of Polly Dunbar to be identified as author/illustrator
of this work has been asserted by her in accordance with
the Copyright, Designs and Patents Act 1988.

This book has been typeset in Gill Sans MT Schoolbook.

Printed in China.

British Library Cataloguing in Publication Data:
a catalogue record for this book is available
from the British Library.

ISBN 978-1-4063-0904-1

www.walker.co.uk

Tilly and
her friends
all live
together in
a little yellow
house...

Pretty
Pru

Polly Dunbar

WALKER BOOKS
AND SUBSIDIARIES
LONDON • BOSTON • SYDNEY • AUCKLAND

"Oh pretty,"
said Pru,
"I'm so pretty!"

She was

putting on her

favourite

red lipstick.

"Can I have some make-up?" said Tumpty.

"Then I can be pretty like you."

"No,"
said Pru.
"You'll
waste it."

"Humpf," said Tumpty.

So while Pru
was busy doing
a pretty-
prance ...

Tumpty stretched out his very
long trunk and took Pru's handbag!

"Look, everybody," said Tumpty.

"Now we can be pretty like Pru."

"Tilly, Tilly, Tilly,"

Pru called.

"My handbag,

it's lost."

"Don't worry," said Tilly.

"It can't be far away."

"Hello, Hector,"
said Tilly.
"Pru's lost
her handbag.
Do you
have it?"

"No," said Hector.

"My handbag!"
cried Pru,
"my green
handbag
with red
spots.

Tiptoe,
have you seen it?"

Tiptoe blushed

the prettiest shade of pink.

"Doodle!"
flapped Pru.
"Have you
seen my
handbag ...

with my blusher
and nail varnish?"

"It wasn't me!" said Doodle,
and she pointed a very pretty finger.

She was
pointing at
Tumpty.

Tumpty was doing
a pretty-prance
of his own.

He looked **extremely funny.**

Everybody laughed ...

everybody except Pru.

"That's **my handbag** on your head," said Pru.

Everybody

stopped laughing.

"I'm sorry,"

Tumpty said.

With a curl of his very long trunk,
he gave Pru her handbag back.

"We're
sorry too,"
said
Hector.

And they put the make-up back in the bag.

Then Pru did
something very special.
She gave Tumpty
her **favourite** red lipstick.

Tumpty did something
very special too...

He let
everybody
have a go ...

and they all pranced prettily,

just like Pru.

The End